CTHULHU PASSANT

CTHULHU PASSANT

Edited by

Travis Heermann

Bear Paw Publishing
Denver

Cover and Interior Illustrations: Chaz Kemp

PAPERBACK EDITION

ISBN 978-1-62225-410-1

Bear Paw Publishing
Denver, Colorado, USA

www.bearpawpublishing.com

CONTENTS

DEDICATION

All proceeds from this book go to the support of women whose lives have been affected by addiction and domestic violence. The horrors to be found within this book hold little comparison to theirs.

The beneficiary of these proceeds is Asbury House, a shelter and care organization in Fort Collins, Colorado. For more information about who they are and what they do, go to asburyhouse.org.

INTRODUCTION

S trange things can happen at conventions when authors get together.

A group of writers sits around in the hotel bar, talking about stories, careers, gossip, talking about H.P. Lovecraft, talking about chess, and then suddenly talking about Lovecraftian chess stories or chess-Lovecraft stories.

And then somebody makes a bet, issues a challenge: to write such a story in a week.

And then we'll vote on the stories, and the writer with the best story "wins" the chance to publish them as an anthology.

And we'll publish it for charity.

And it will benefit women's shelters and programs for victims of domestic violence.

So we did it, it happened, and here I am, having won for myself a ton of work and the privilege of putting together this selection of stories by some excellent writers. I'm honored to share these pages with the work of three Bram Stoker Award nominees, the writers Guy Anthony De Marco and Peter J. Wacks, plus the artistic talents of Chaz Kemp, who collaborated with them on their nominated graphic novel, *Behind These Eyes*. And the other writers ain't no slouches either. Vivian Caethe's collection *Handwritten* is a delectable smorgasbord of flash fiction and crunchy vignettes. Sam Knight's short stories are starting to spread like wildfire to other anthologies like *Penny Dread Tales III*.

I am also privileged to be able to support a worthy charity with this effort in a time when support for women's organizations seems to be under attack at every level of society from a vocal, strident minority

that seems bent on dragging women's rights back into the 19th century.
I like the idea of hope coming from horror.

The title of this anthology comes from a particular chess move where one pawn can take another pawn *en passant*, or "in passing."

The French word *passant* can also be used to mean "passerby". Great Cthulhu, Lovecraft's timeless Great Old One, could destroy us *en passant* with a shrug of his slimy wing from his dreaming place beneath the Pacific Ocean.

In these stories come brushes with the cosmic, the unfathomable, the unspeakable mysteries of the universe, coupled with what is arguably the greatest game ever devised on this blue ball spinning through the void. What better metaphor for the cosmic, the unknowable, than a game with more possibilities than there are quarks in this universe?

And from that cosmic mystery comes ... what?
Cthulhu ftaghn.

Travis Heermann
April, 2014

"And Knight takes pawn, E5." Toby looked up from the chessboard, a large smile spread across his brown face. "This opening is pretty ancient. Your move."

Sarah scanned the board, her dark eyes jerking as though she were in a deep REM sleep. She closed them and yawned, then stretched her arms until they touched the roof of the 1978 Dodge camper van and her shoulders made a small popping sound. "We're supposed to be camping and having fun on our first date. You promised fun. I distinctly remember that word. Chess is as fun as watching professional miniature golf." She dropped her arms back down. "Stupid name for an opening move anyway, Fried Liver Attack. I'm stuck, I don't know where to move next, and I'd rather be kissing you right about now."

Toby smiled, then puckered up.

After a few minutes, they broke apart. Sarah blushed and giggled. "My father would be so pissed right now. 'You shouldn't be alone in the middle of nowhere with that stranger.'" Her brow furrowed. "Of course, a stranger means someone who isn't white." She sighed and put her hand on Toby's. "Old school, old fool when it comes to race relations. You'll have to remember that when you meet him."

"Already planning to introduce me to your family, eh?" With his other hand, he rubbed Sarah's knuckles. "I could tell him I'm set up with a lucrative tech support job with IBM once I graduate."

"No, that would make things worse. It's not the money, it's the stereotype." She lowered her voice an octave and said in a mock Indian accent, "Hello, my name is Samuel L. Jackson, how may I fix your computer today?"

"Well, I guess I won't tell him my father owns a chain of 7-11's," Toby replied. "Icing on the cake. Speaking of cake, there's some snacks in the cooler. Hungry?"

"Starving."

Toby struggled with the side door for a few moments until it slid open, squealing in rusty protest. They hopped out of the recreational vehicle and stretched, followed by a few fumbling kisses.

"You want a beer?"

"Eh, why not," said Sarah. "Got anything substantial in there too?"

Toby walked over to a cooler mounted on a shelf connected to the towing hitch on the back of the RV. He toyed with the bungee cords and opened the top. "Substantial, yes. Nourishing, that's a gamble." He handed two Budweiser longnecks to Sarah, who twisted off the caps. He dug around and pulled out a couple of sandwiches and a box of Twinkies.

"Tuna or turkey?" he asked.

"Turkey. I don't want tuna breath."

Toby exchanged a sandwich and a couple of Twinkies for a longneck. "You'll get tuna breath anyway if you keep smooching me."

"Okay, I guess I'll have to stop kissing you then." She playfully raised an eyebrow and smirked.

"Prefer you didn't," he said. "Come on, let's finish that game and we can go on a hike."

Sarah looked around the small clearing they had found on an old logging road. "These trees don't look too happy that we're here." Even though it was sunny, she felt a cold chill that gave her goose bumps.

The clearing looked like it was created by a meteor strike. The ground had no dirt, just bare granite in the shape of a circle. The trees leaned away, as though they were afraid to grow over the spot.

"Actually, the trees are all bunched together like they're a barrier," she said. "I wonder if someone planted them that way?"

Toby turned to look at the circle. "Yeah, I see what you mean. Look at how they're all dead-looking on this side, but they're green on the other."

Sarah shuddered with another cold chill. "I hope I'm not coming down with something. Let's go in. I need my sweater."

After climbing back into the Dodge, Toby forced the sliding door closed.

"Oh, it's nice and toasty in here!" said Sarah. "Is the heater on?"

"Nope, it's busted," Toby replied. "Maybe the sun is hitting the roof just right. Let's continue the game, shall we?"

"We can, but I need to check my blood sugar."

Toby raised an eyebrow. "I didn't know you were diabetic."

"There's lots of things you don't know about me," she replied as she dug her glucose meter out of her purse. "Isn't that the point of having a first date?"

"Well, yeah, but we've been friends for three years."

Sarah loaded a lancet and pressed the trigger to prick the finger she had wiped with an alcohol pad. "I don't know, I just don't like people to know. They think I'm defective or something because I was born this way." She squeezed her fingertip until a small sphere of blood appeared. She slid a test strip into the meter and dipped the tip into the blood. "I got bullied when I was in kindergarten."

"Let me take the TARDIS and go back in time to kick their asses."

"Heh, right. One's a preacher, and the other is a middleweight mixed martial arts champion," she said. "OK, good. Little low at 87, so I'm cleared for Twinkie consumption."

Toby thought for a second. "That preacher will never know what hit him. But seriously, talk to me when you have something important to say."

"I will. Oh, shit," said Sarah. "I got some blood on the chessboard. I'm sorry."

"No worries. It's old, and it has plenty of scars and stains," said Toby. "I was told it was my grandfather's set. He was nuts, and ended up getting shot by the police in Mumbai, back when it was called Bombay. He killed a bunch of people with a *khukuri*." He saw the puzzled look on Sarah's face. "It's a forward-curved knife, pretty nasty. Took out over sixty people. It was quite the scandal. He kept screaming about getting the demons out of their bodies."

"Okay, enough with the crazy talk. I'll move this pawn."

Toby smiled. "Surprisingly astute move. Maybe you're really a ringer and you're playing with my head." He countered with his own pawn.

"Why so shocked?" mocked Sarah in a sing-song voice, fluttering her eyes and acting demure. "Afraid of getting beaten by a girl?"

Toby opened his mouth to reply, but a movement from the front of the camper caught his attention. "What the ..."

Sarah opened her eyes and followed Toby's gaze.

A black, rubbery-looking arm slowly stretched out from under the driver's seat towards them. The skin had an alligator texture with oozing burn scabs. The cracks in the skin glowed, flashing a dim ember-red. The appendage was capped by a long-fingered hand with spiky black nails. Toby and Sarah watched it reach between them and move Sarah's knight to take a pawn. The hand retracted in slow motion until it merged with the darkness under the seat, leaving a stench like a steaming, road-kill funeral pyre.

Toby looked across the board at his opponent's shocked face. "That has got to be the most fucked-up thing I've ever experienced."

Sarah twisted in her seat to reach her longneck. "Holy shit, did you put something in my beer?"

He looked appalled. "Of course I didn't. You opened the bottles."

Shaking her long, brown hair from her face, Sarah bent over low to peer under the seat. The darkness was an event horizon. "I don't see anything under there." She put one of her cheeks on the floor. "I can't see through to where the gas pedal is, so there's something blocking it. Go see what it is."

"Like Hell I will," said Toby. "Besides, it must've been a shadow or a big moth or something." He cocked his head to the side. "But ... I thought I saw a tentacle or an arm, you?"

Sarah nodded. "An arm. It was really gross looking. A shared hallucination?"

"Must be. Something like that thing can't possibly exist." He straightened his head while Sarah sat back down. "We must be on the same wavelength if we imagined the same thing."

"Yeah. Yeah, you're right. Creepy." She pursed her lips as she looked at the chessboard. "That knight did move, though."

Toby giggled half-heartedly and turned his attention back to the chessboard. Ignoring her observation, he said, "OK, now we'll move this pawn up two squares."

Sarah didn't bother to watch his move. She kept watching the dark space under the driver's seat and inhaled sharply when she saw something stir.

The same arm pushed its way outward, as though it was struggling through a membrane separating the dark from the sunlit area of the van. Small flakes of ash cracked off and landed on the worn, rose-colored carpet as the arm stretched across the empty space between the chair and the chess players, who sat frozen with panicked expressions. Again, the thin, elongated fingers selected a chess piece, moving a pawn forward one square. The hand lingered for a few seconds, gliding over the rest of the chess board, before the arm retracted to the shadow.

Sarah started babbling, tears glistening on her cheeks. "Oh, my God. Oh, my God." She pointed towards the front of the van. "Did you see that, as it was going away?"

Toby shook his head, still in shock, muttering, "It can't be real ... it *can't* be real ..."

"That ... that thing has fucking eyes on the tips of the fingers." She trembled uncontrollably, rubbing the goose bumps on her pale arms. "What is it? *What kind of thing has eyes on its fucking fingertips?*"

"Maybe it's carbon monoxide poisoning." Toby jumped up, startling Sarah. "We're outta here. C'mon." He grabbed the side door handle and tugged hard.

The handle snapped off. As he looked at the end of the connecting bar, he could see the metal cooling as though it had recently been subjected to a plasma torch. Toby showed it to Sarah, who started sobbing.

"We ha-ha-have to get out of here, we're going to die if we don't."

Toby nodded towards the front. "The driver's and passenger's side doors are the only other ways outta here."

Sarah shrank back, a look of revulsion on her face. "No way. No fucking way. That thing is still under the seat."

"Well," said Toby, "it's either stay here or make a run for it."

Sarah nodded. Toby grabbed her wrists and held them tight against his chest until she stopped shaking and steeled herself for an escape.

Guy Anthony De Marco

He turned towards the front when something new distracted him. "It's three o'clock in the afternoon, why is it getting dark out?"

Sarah pushed aside the thick curtain covering the large, sealed window over the tiny, single-bowl sink and screamed.

Thousands of black, yellow, and red insects crawled over the safety glass, a chaotic cloud of predatory bugs. Thick-abdomen wasps pushed their way through a blanket of hornets, bees, and common flies. The light grew dimmer as the mass of roiling creatures also spread over the front windshield.

"We're trapped," said Toby, a maniacal look of desperation spread across his features. "I'm allergic to bees."

Sarah wiped the tears from her face and angrily punched him in the arm. "Why did you take me camping on an Indian burial ground?"

"My family's from India, not American Indian. What are we going to do? We can't get ..." He grabbed Sarah's shoulder and pointed at the front seats.

The hand was back, although this time the cracks seemed to glow brighter with the windows mostly blocked. It was pointing at the chess board.

Toby had an epiphany. "It's like Harry Potter. We have to play to get out."

"Well, you're the chess champion," said Sarah. "I'm just the soccer jock. You play against it."

They sat together on the side with the white pieces, facing the disembodied arm.

"I noticed it's playing the correct countermoves to the Fried Liver Attack. I'm going to have to improvise."

"Do what you have to do. I promise I'll never call you a geek in front of the soccer team again." Sarah squeezed Toby's hand for encouragement. "I know you can win."

They began to play in earnest. After an hour passed, Toby was missing enough pieces that he knew he wouldn't win, but he couldn't bring himself to tell Sarah. Each time Toby lost a chess token, the hand would convulse as though it was laughing.

"It's getting hotter in here," Sarah finally said. She could sense things weren't going well. "That arm thing is putting out a lot of heat."

Toby looked up from the board and realized the cracks were oozing an angry red light like lava spewing from a volcano. "Damn, it's getting stronger the more we play." He moved his bishop to take the creature's queen-side rook, but the victory was short-lived. Toby was placed in check, and he realized he had to sacrifice his queen to escape.

"Oh, shit." Sarah pointed to the driver's seat, which was now engulfed in a black sphere where no light escaped. Another arm was pushing through, this one with a wide mouth on the palm, a gash filled with rows of inward-pointing needle sharp teeth. As soon as it cleared the sphere it began to hiss and groan, as though a graveyard full of souls were being tormented in its belly. The horrible stench of burning dead flesh hung in the van like a low, stifling cloud. The two arms emitted so much heat that Toby and Sarah were soaked with sweat. The glowing cracks were making a sizzling sound, and little drops of molten ichor dripped off the arms, melting the polyester carpet in spots.

"I can't win this," Toby finally admitted. "I have maybe three or four moves left, tops. The key to this game is to maybe get it into a draw."

"Wait," said Sarah. "It's getting stronger as we play, right?"

"Yeah, so?"

"*That's* the key. Why not do this?" Sarah reached out and tipped the white king over, a signal of defeat.

"What have you done?" Toby cried, pulling out chunks of his sweaty hair.

The arms began to flail around, shredding the furniture and walls of the RV. Sarah and Toby backed up as far as possible, just out of their reach.

A keening wail from the mouth of the second arm pierced the air as the entity was sucked back into the shrinking sphere of nothingness. As it disappeared with a pop, the insects on the windows, no longer mesmerized, lazily flew off in random directions.

"How did you do that?" asked Toby. "No, wait. *Why* did you do it? That was crazy risky!"

Sarah smiled. "I thought it was using the chess board and the game as a key to open a portal. The more we played, the stronger it got. The black bubble it came from also got big enough to let something horrible through. I ended the game before the final tumbler could click."

Toby reached over and pulled Sarah into an embrace. "That was a flash of brilliance and insight."

"I know," she said, and kissed him.

They picked their way over the wreckage of the ruined RV, kicking open the side door that the arms had weakened with their final tantrum.

The clearing appeared to be freshly scorched, the surrounding trees smoked from being exposed to a massive heat source. A ring of freshly charred insects encircled Toby's ruined van.

They stood in the clearing for several minutes, holding hands and blankly staring at the scene.

Sarah broke the silence. "You need to teach me chess."

Toby pulled out his Zippo lighter, flicked the wheel until it lit, and tossed it into the rear of the Dodge. After a few minutes, heavy smoke heaved out of the wound in its side.

"No way I'll teach you chess. With your insight, I'll never beat you again." Toby put his arm around her shoulder and started off towards the trail back to the highway.

"Again? You haven't beaten me yet." She pecked him on the cheek. "But I'd settle for a tie."

Guy Anthony De Marco is a speculative fiction author; a Graphic Novel Bram Stoker Award® finalist; winner of the HWA Silver Hammer Award; a prolific short story and flash fiction crafter; a novelist; an invisible man with superhero powers; a game writer (Sojourner Tales modules, Interface Zero 2.0 core team, D&D modules); and a coffee addict. One of these is false.

A writer since 1977, Guy is a member of the following organizations: SFWA, WWA, SFPA, IAMTW, ASCAP, RMFW, NCW, HWA. He hopes to collect the rest of the letters of the alphabet one day. Additional information can be found at Wikipedia, GuyAndTonya.com, and GuyAnthonyDeMarco.com.

Guy knows where a similar, barren circle is located in the Adirondack Mountains. The arms he saw in a nightmare when he was three years old.

THE ISOLATED PAWN

Sam Knight

The old man sat in the dusty underground cavern, his face lit by the glow of a single small candle. He sat on an old, steel milk crate, facing a small travel chessboard upon a stack of three tires. The chessboard and the small candles, of which several had already been used up, had been his only companions for four days—at least, the only companions other than the chanting voices in his head. He guessed it had been four days, as he had slept four times since his interment. Time had been lost since fleeing to this place, since the creatures had destroyed the Earth above.

He couldn't imagine what the world above must look like now. There had been videos and images broadcast from other cities, as they were leveled before the advancing beasts, but those *mere images* had been nothing next to the horrific blares of the trumpets heralding the End Times that had come from above once the monsters reached his home city of Tashkent.

When the blaring noise began, the dust in the cavern rose off the ground as one formed cloud sent dancing by the force of the impacts shaking the earth.

The old man had waited for the top of the cavern to come down upon him, to crush him between its stalagmite and stalactite teeth, but it hadn't. Instead the darkness had swallowed him whole, and now he waited to die within its hollow gullet.

The noises above faded away not long after the attack upon the city started. There had been sirens: air raid sirens, police sirens, ambulance sirens, the sirens of wailing women and children and men. Too many sirens. And then the earth-shattering growls and roars. Sounds so deep, from voices so vast, that the physical world could not stand against them, and buildings crumbled before them.

It lasted an eternity.

When it stopped, the old man thought he had gone deaf, but he could no longer feel it in his bones either.

There could be no city left above him. He doubted there could be anything left up there. He found no reason in trying to dig his way out of the cave. It was as good a place to die as any.

He idly wondered which beast had destroyed his city as he stared at the chess game in the flickering light.

There were two leviathans, according to the reports. Both nightmarishly grotesque bastardizations of the cephalopod's form. One resembling some sort of bizarre bipedal squid with too many tentacles, the other less squid-like, the old man thought, and more an octopus with wings, yet it also had too many tentacles.

Many who looked upon the creatures went mad, even when only viewing the ungodly visages through pre-recorded images on electronic devices. Idiots now, they shuffled like the undead through the street muttering a chant in unison. *Ph'nglui mgnilgh'ri Cthulhu ah'shugg c'bthnk.*

Others, although retaining their sanity, lost their capacity for reasoning to an unbridled, defecating fear. Everyone *knew* the creatures to be of the Old Ones. There was no denying it, questioning it, or attempting to reason. It just was, and when your very soul shuddered with knowledge, you knew.

The old man sometimes thought that he might remember his name. It would flicker across the edge of his consciousness like a moth passing by in the dark. Then he would think better of it. He preferred not to think of himself at all. He had allowed himself to become part of whatever was left of the rest of the world, a unified part with no individuality. And he liked it this way. It was better this way. It was easier to ignore the chanting voices in his head this way.

The effect of the monsters' arrival had been an unparalleled plague against humanity. Within hours half of the population of Earth had gone mad, either with the mindless chanting, or screaming in terror. Yet the two beasts had hardly moved.

According to the reports the old man had seen, one of the creatures had fallen from out of the darkness beyond the heavens. As if in answer, the other, the one less squid-like, had risen from the unknown depths of the ocean. The creatures had started on opposite ends of the continent and slowly worked toward the center, where the old man lived. He assumed it was just a coincidence that his beloved Uzbekistan should be their meeting place. That people or places below their feet meant anything to the beasts was unfathomable.

They seemed only to move one at a time, stopping and holding still—unnaturally still, waiting for the other creature to move and stop before continuing on again. The behemoths took turns destroying cities, effortlessly laying waste to all around them. It had taken nearly a month for them to reach the center of the continent. Behind them lie a seemingly random pattern of destruction, wherein some cities had been leveled, leaving little more than a bare spot upon the earth to indicate anything ever existed, while other cities were left completely untouched, save for the poor souls whose sanity fled.

Humans had used every weapon at their disposal on the beasts, to no avail. Scorched, irradiated, poisoned land remained behind where the Old Ones passed.

The old man reached toward the chessboard, but hesitated as he considered. He had played many games against himself over the last few days. Too many. There was nothing else for him to do, except perhaps claw his own eyes out. An option he still occasionally considered. The entrance to the cavern had been sealed shut during the razing of the city above him. He had brought food and water with him, but he had lost most of it during a time of non-existence brought on by the unholy cacophony of sound that had assaulted him from above. He knew he was going to die in this cave, but didn't have enough will remaining to bring his waiting to an end.

So he stared at the chessboard.

The little magnetic pieces had begun to take on personalities to him. One of the white knights had a scratch across the top of the horse's eye. He had come to think of this one as the rakish rogue, the one who would do anything for the love of his queen, regardless of what the king may think. One of the black castles was chipped on top, leaving a gaping hole in the crenellations. He often felt this piece could not properly defend itself. Two of the pawns, both black, had a nubbin left from an improperly trimmed molding. These often seemed to him to be brothers working together.

It was one of these black pawns he moved first, out from in front of the king, taking the full two squares. The old man thought to free the queen and the bishop early this game. The black pawn seemed sad to see his brother move on without him, but the rest of the black pieces seemed to cheer that they had moved first, grateful to the old man for giving up on the rule that white always got to go first.

The man rotated the board to play the white pieces. They seemed sullen, chagrined that he had snubbed them and allowed black to open the game.

"We can't just do the same thing over and over again, now can we?" His voice echoed through the cave as he answered his silent accusers.

Reaching for a white pawn, his hand wavered.

White no longer wanted to play.

Defiantly, the pieces turned their backs on him and refused to be a part of the game.

"You can't do that." The man frowned. He looked around anxiously. "You have to play."

White refused.

The old man grabbed for one of the white pawns and moved it. It was neither the pawn he had reached for, nor did it land where he had intended to place it. A smugness came over White. The old man could force them to move, but he could not control their move.

He had reached for the pawn in front of the castle on his right, the one with the broken defenses, thinking that he would use the castle quickly, before it was breached. Instead, he had moved the pawn in front of the bishop and placed it so that the black pawn could easily take it the next move, as well as get out of the way of the queen, freeing her to wreak havoc across the board.

He turned the board to Black's point of view. The black pawn's brother was cheering. "Take him! Take him!"

The old man considered. If the black pawn took the white pawn, that opened the whole board up. If the black pawn didn't move, if he brought his queen out instead, then White could capture it next move, sacrificing itself to the queen. If he allowed the brother to take the white pawn ... What was White up to?

The old man gave in to the jeering of the black pawn's brother and took the white pawn.

For a moment, the cheering of Black at the taking of first blood drowned out the chanting in the back of the old man's thoughts. Noticing the lack of imposition into his mind of the chanting brought it rebounding back stronger than before.

Ph'nglui mgnilgh'ri Cthulhu ah'shugg c'bthnk.

He could feel the changes that had taken place in the world. The presence of things not right, not comprehensible. The chanting in his head brought them closer, made them tangible, put them in the cave with him. He knew they were there, but he couldn't allow himself to look at them. He couldn't allow himself to go mad that way. He took a couple of deep breaths and forced himself to relax, becoming one with the world around him again.

When he felt like he wasn't going to spin out of control, he turned the board to see what White's game was. White had imitated his opening move, bringing out the pawn from in front of the king, placing it alongside the victorious black brother.

"En passant! En passant!" Black cheered for its pawn to step behind the White piece and take it in passing.

The old man spun the board back around and eyed it suspiciously. He licked his dry lips and remembered he was out of water. He pushed the thought aside and stared at the playing field.

Distraction would bring the things in the cave closer, would cost him his sanity.

Why had White done that? This was not the move of someone thinking ahead! This game was going to be over very quickly ... unless White *had* thought ahead.

White was trying to bait him, trying to lead him into a trap! If the black pawn took the white pawn, the white queen would come out and do just as he had intended for Black all along.

Ignoring the cries of the Black pieces, the old man left the black

19

pawn where it was, giving up the right of *en passant,* and instead he slid the black queen on the diagonal all the way to the edge of the board, putting the white king in check.

"Check!" he announced satisfied. White would have to move the pawn out from in front of the knight to block the black queen and thus spare its king.

But that's not what it did.

Instead, the white king stepped forward one space.

The white queen gasped, but her resolve held her stiffly in place. The white knight with the scar over his eye glanced nervously from his love to his sovereign.

All of the white pieces on the board indifferently ignored the old man, uncaring about his shocked reaction as he closely examined the move and considered the implications.

Black called for blood, the brother of the pawn already out screaming loudest of all. The old man listened intently to the pawn screaming at him. Anything was better than acknowledging the presence in the cave with him. Finally the old man allowed the black pawn to take his two squares.

White's king calmly took one diagonal step forward and faced the newcomer across an empty square.

The old man's eyes widened as he finally realized White's strategy. Murmurs and exclamations of shock came up from Black's side of the board. White wasn't just playing defiantly. White was playing to lose.

"You can't do that ..." the old man muttered. He stood up and paced a circle behind his milk crate. "You can't do that!" His dry voice cracked hoarsely, echoing down the cavern like the dying roar of a lion.

White mocked him.

"It doesn't matter if you don't want to play! You have to!" The old man pulled at his hair in frustration. "You have to! I can force you to play!"

But he knew he couldn't force White to try to win.

What was the point in playing if not to win?

He paced back and forth, muttering, pulling at his hair, biting his lip. How could this be? White had to play. But white didn't have to try to win ....

The old man had no idea how long ago the candle had guttered out. It was the smoke from the extinguished wick that brought him out of his reverie. The smell seemed old and stale. His swollen tongue seemed too big for his mouth. He suspected that he had been pacing for hours. Why wasn't it dark?

Fear rose up inside of him as he began to consider the loss of his sanity.

The fear grew stronger as he worried what he would see, were he to allow his sanity to creep back into his thoughts, to consider things best left ignored.

There was no need to be afraid when he was one with everything. He needed to not be again. He lay down on the floor of the cavern, curled himself into a ball, and slept, dreaming of great battles planned out eons in advance, and unwilling participants refusing to try to win.

Ph *'nglui mgnilgh'ri Cthulhu ah'shugg c'bthnk.*
The chant haunted the old man's dreams.
Ph'nglui mgnilgh'ri Cthulhu ah'shugg c'bthnk.
He was on the verge of understanding it. It called to him as the moisture dripping into his mouth woke him with more agony than relief, stinging and burning the cracks in his tongue and lips. The liquid had a strange odor, but taste was beyond the old man's ability.

His eyes were dry and grated in their sockets. As he focused on the creature above him, his autonomic reflexes attempted to vacate his bladder and bowels, but they were already empty.

The giant, bioluminescent, blubbery grub-worm towering over him should have driven him out of his mind, but his sanity had already fled.

The creature, larger than a bus, filled most of the cavern. Its bloated body pulsated with pustules that filled and shrank like the slow-motion boiling of water. Eyes, glowing sickly green, appeared and disappeared from its roiling hide, and some pseudopodial appendage was dripping the liquid into his mouth through an ovoid sphincter at the tip.

The old man gagged and retched as his body tried to reject the oily, citrus- and sulfur-flavored lactation, but his body was too weak.

Ph'nglui mgnilgh'ri Cthulhu ah'shugg c'bthnk.

Even from beyond, Cthulhu devours the realm of Earth and our essence.

The shoggoth waited.

The old man had his strength back. The liquids and solids forced into his mouth by the shoggoth had rejuvenated his body's strength, if nothing else. The mere presence of the creature had driven his sanity further away, let alone any realization of what it had been doing to him.

He wished for the return of the darkness, so that he would no longer have to see the wretched creature. Once, the thought of clawing his own eyes out settled firmly into the old man's mind. The beast restrained him with tentacle-like pseudopods until he passed out from screaming.

The shoggoth waited.

"What do you want with me?" The old man screamed at the creature for the hundredth time. He had become inured enough to try punching the creature. His hands sunk into the viscous flesh, and he felt them being gently sucked on, pulling him closer. Retching, he pulled away and passed out in the farthest reaches of the cavern, as far away from the creature as he could get.

When he awoke, the creature was feeding him again.

He no longer tried to sleep, for fear of being fed.

The shoggoth waited.

The old man knew the shoggoth was of the Old Ones above. He could feel their presence in it enough to know that it was a shoggoth, and that it was under their control.

Out of desperation, the man returned to his chessboard. He had not thought of it since the creature had arrived. He had no way of knowing how long ago that had been. Days, months? Even his beard was no indication. The oozing liquids the shoggoth spilled all over him as it fed him had removed all of his body hair.

He picked up the expended candle from next to the chessboard and sniffed at the burnt wick. The waxy, smoky smell washed over him in a wave of heavenly grace, memories of a time when his world was not filled with the shoggoth.

He sat the candle down and examined the board.

The white king was in danger. He had been attempting to sacrifice himself. White had been playing to lose.

Anger at the betrayal rose again. He turned to pace behind his milk crate and found the shoggoth had moved close in behind him. At least fifty eyes were on him and the chess board.

The monstrosity oozed back a few feet and gave the man room.

The man took it and began walking a small circle. Out of the corner of his eye, he could see the white queen defiantly holding her chin high and refusing to look at him. The king stood stoically facing off against one of the black pawn brothers.

What to do?

He could quickly end the game, let White lose. But then what of the next game? White would just lose again. And again. There was nothing to be had by that.

Black had to play to lose, too, to balance the efforts, or the game would be moot.

He strode over to the board and, ignoring the screaming protests of Black, slid the black queen diagonally to the square vacated by the white king.

The two queens stood side by side, refusing to look at one another.

The white king stepped back, in front of the black queen and dared her to usurp him.

Black cheered and called for their monarch to finish the battle. Instead, the old man convinced the first black pawn to step forward and block the white king in, so that he could no longer put himself into danger.

Disgruntled, the pawn agreed.

Without warning, the white knight with the scar sprang upon the pawn, taking him down in one demolishing pounce.

Cries of outrage rose as Black called for vengeance. The pawn's brother took out the white pawn that had been standing beside his brother for so long.

23

Even as Black gloated, the old man could feel White's smugness. It knew it still controlled the situation.

The rogue knight leapt again, and Black's queen went down.

Out of sheer rage, the brother stomped up to glare in the white king's face. The desire to destroy coming from him was palpable, but the king was not in his kill zone.

Tensions had gotten so high the old man jumped up from his milk crate and pushed at the flabby, bubbling bulk of the shoggoth, making room for himself to pace.

What was White's game? Was White really playing to lose? Or playing to win? Had White changed strategies?

He reflexively reached up to pull at his hair, but he no longer had any. Frustrated, he knocked his knuckles against his bald pate in a rhythmic fashion.

The shoggoth waited.

Ph'nglui mgnilgh'ri Cthulhu ah'shugg c'bthnk.

The chanting in his skull grew greater as he allowed himself to feel the emotions, allowed himself to have individuality apart from his surroundings. He feared the growing call of the chant inside him, and that enraged him even further. He was sick of being afraid. He was tired of being insane. He wanted his name back.

He went into a rage and attacked the shoggoth, swinging his fists futilely at the living vileness.

Ph'nglui mgnilgh'ri Cthulhu ah'shugg c'bthnk.

Ph'nglui mgnilgh'ri Cthulhu ah'shugg c'bthnk.

Even from beyond, Cthulhu devours the realm of Earth and our essence.

How long he had been chanting the words he could not guess. That he was no longer chanting them was a shock to his system.

He was sitting on the milk crate, staring at the chessboard when he came to his senses. Or what was left of them.

Black was screaming for vengeance.

White was .... He didn't know what White was doing. White was no longer smug, yet it was also no longer ... anything. White had become nothing but pieces on the board.

And Black pressed him to take the advantage, to push on while

White was not there, was not watching.

"But that is no game at all," he muttered. "This is worse than White not playing by the rules .... This leaves us all alone."

Black fell silent as it considered his words, and then it too went away.

For the first time since entering the cavern, the old man felt truly alone. He turned to look at the shoggoth, wondering at the lack of feelings he felt for it.

He no longer feared the beast. He no longer felt anything at all.

Without the game, he had nothing. He was nothing.

Kadishtu c'k'yarnak.

Knowledge has been granted.

The shoggoth inched past the old man like a cutworm, forcing its bulbous mass out through the caved-in entrance, displacing tons of rock as it went. As it moved out and away into the ruins of Earth, sickly yellow sunlight filtered weakly into the cavern.

Weak though it was, the light seared the man's eyes. He stumbled after the creature, knowing now what it had wanted.

No. The shoggoth was only a vessel, a messenger. The old man now knew what Cthulhu had wanted of him. It had wanted him to understand.

He looked out over the desolate lands where once a great city had stood, and knew he had found his new game. He would find what was left of the human race and try to explain to them that they were, had always been, nothing more than pawns in a game that they could not possibly understand. And yet, without the game, they were nothing.

Sam Knight, a Colorado native, spent ten years in California's wine country before returning to the Rockies. When asked if he misses California, he gets a wistful look in his eyes and replies he misses the green mountains in the winter, but he is glad to be back home.

He claims to still be able to remember the look, feel, and smell of some books, and has been spotted sniffing books as he ruffles the pages. Once upon a time, he was known to quote books the way some people quote movies, but now he claims having a family has made him forgetful, as a survival adaptation.

As a writer, Sam refuses to be pinned down into a genre and writes whatever grabs his attention, be it horror, children's books, or a Cthulhu chess story. Sam's inspiration for the story in this anthology came from remembering what it was like to play chess alone, as a child, when he used the pieces to make up stories more than to play.

He has spoken at Denver and Salt Lake City Comic Cons, as well as numerous smaller conventions, and is part of the production team at WordFire Press. Sam can be found at SamKnight.com and contacted at sam@samknight.com.

IN THE MOVE OF MADNESS

Peter J. Wacks

1936

Antarctica

"**O**UTER SEAL INITIATED. SPECIMEN DETECTED.**"** The soft feminine voice came from the air, disembodied.

Gases pumped into the chamber, designed to debilitate the mind of any intruder on the ship's bridge. "META-STABILITY DRIVE DAMAGE CRITICAL. PLEASE ENTER SEAL UNLOCK SEQUENCE TO ACCESS CENTRAL DATABANKS." The room's occupant stood dazed as the grid at his feet lit up.

Person by person, the room emptied. Two players sat across from each other, board untouched. Quiet filled the space. White faced black across empty battlefield. Soon enough it would be filled. Fighting the tension, each stared at the board, imagining the possibilities of the game that would unfold. Each player would start with one of twenty possible moves, by the fourth move there were almost seventy two thousand possible games they might be playing.

e4

'Click' went the clock.

... e6

'Click' went the clock.

Moisture welled on Tim's forehead, sweat dripped. He reached forward tentatively, chose his piece, moved.

d3

'Click' went the clock.

The player sitting across the board smiled. There was no humor, no friendliness to the smile. Exposed teeth were feral. Surely it was a trick of the light, but his skin seemed to have a green tint.

... d5

'Click' went the clock.

Tim was afraid, something he had never felt sitting at the chessboard. This match, the Romanian national finals, should be a no brainer. There wasn't another player in the Carpathian Mountains who could match him. Bile soured his mouth. Why was he afraid?

Nd2

'Click' went the clock.

His opponent was an unknown—Sterling Romanovich. The man was sickly thin, reminding Tim of a praying mantis

... Nf6

'Click' went the clock.

Tim paused. His opponent was mirroring his defense. Not a strong opening. A drop of sweat dripped onto his notation book. Why couldn't he collect his thoughts?

g3 ... c5

'Click, click' went the clock.

Tim reached forward to move another pawn and paused. His fingers were slick, his hand shaking. It moved of its own accord, to a different piece.

Bg2

'Click' went the clock.

He blinked. Why had he just reversed his strategy and played into an Indian? Eyes met across the board, Tim sank into his opponent's stare. Was it a trick, of were Sterling's irises faintly red? Tim blinked. He blinked again. He was playing a man. Just a man. There was nothing more happening here ... he was just psyching himself out, buckling under the pressure of his first championship.

... Nc6

'Click' went the clock.

"Thank you for giving me the offensive, friend." Sterling licked his teeth and reached forward.

Ngf3

'Click' went the clock.

"Uh ..." Wiping at the sweat with his left hand, Tim was surprised to discover his skin was dry. "You are an amateur, my friend. You reveal a certain shortsightedness." Psychology was important on the board, even if the barb lacked any depth. Tim refused to let the man across from him see him crumbling.

... Be7 'Click' went the clock.

Since he had started, might as well finish the Indian structure, otherwise he would be wasting tempo.

0-0 'Click' went the clock.

Water dripped from rotted walls. Pipes, broken and jagged, showed through holes—corroded teeth trying to bite the world. Footsteps echoed from the dark hallways leading to the chamber. Tim blinked.

He needed to finish building his Indian, sort out where the mid-game battle would occur. Perhaps he could still reveal a center attack, swing the tempo in his favor.

... 0-0 'Click.'

Sterling's eyes narrowed, his smile widened.

e5 'Click.'

Grinding his teeth together, Tim tried to hide frustration. The center was under intense attack, he was already losing control. Perhaps pushing the knight attack would buy time.

... Knd7 'Click.'

Creaking and groaning echoed in the room. The walls moved minutely, masticating the chamber an inch at a time. Something moved by the chambers, a shadow hiding in the shadows.

Re1 'Click.'

Why? Why would he make such a blatantly bad move? Something about this man was forcing Tim into poor choices, bad mind spaces ... into losing. Why would he fumble like this? He had been forced to waste a move protecting his pawn. Or ... maybe there was a way out.

... b5

'Click' went the clock.

Trying to broadcast confidence, Tim met his opponent's eyes. "You are playing to me. Excellent." Time to reassert control of his center, though in a roundabout way.

Knf1 'Click.'

Sterling's lips parted, his sickly smile making Tim sick. "You don't fool me. You don't even know what game you are playing." He slid another piece forward.

... b4 'Click.'

Actinic odors teased Tim's nose, followed by the pungent smell of rotted meat. He looked around at the empty room. There was only a window for the judges to watch, his opponent, and the board. "What is..." he shook his head to clear the cobwebs. "No. I know what I am doing."

h4 'Click.'

"I think it's down this way!" The speaker was far from the chamber.

"Shhh!" another voice replied.

The room was glowing now, shadows around the edge melting beneath an omnipresent green glow, though the center was still dark. Movement bubbled in the play between light and shadow.

"Do you?" Sterling asked casually as he slid another piece across the board.

... b4

'Click' went the clock.

"What?" Tim tried to blink the sweat and confusion out of his eyes. He reached forward but the piece was slick and slightly sticky. There didn't seem to be anything on it ....

'Click' went the clock.

The room pulsated with the sickly glow. Shadows faded with each click that echoed through the chamber. Arcane shapes reached from the center of the room as shadows moved. Every inch revealed stayed empty, failing to be filled with the expected horrors.

Something in the center of the room groaned. Something unearthly, otherworldly. In the groan was a sense of struggle, loss and gain, hopes and nightmares.

"Stop." The lights paused their bobbing progress forward. "Did you hear that, Professor?"

"Indeed I did, young Danforth. Indeed I did. I do not believe that a human made that sound."

'Click' went the clock.

Tim stared at Sterling. Green light emanated from the man's eyes, locking Tim in hypnosis. Pressure pushed against his mind, his soul, the fabric of self, woven together at his core.

He blinked.

He closed his eyes, focusing. Inhale. Exhale. Release the pressure. He scratched at his temple. Inhale. Exhale. Stickiness dripped from his hairline, the pressure was relieved. Choosing carefully, he made his move.

Smoke curled through the air as Sterling took a drag from his cigarette. Tim watched the smoke, confused. When had he lit up?

"Timothy, you seem to be falling to pieces."

"You're not in my head anymore, Sterling. I don't know what you did at the beginning of the game, but it is over now. You will lose."

The opponent slid a piece across the battlefield.

Pressure pushed again, a worm crawling under his temple; a few more scratches relieved it as Tim made his next move. The pieces were becoming clear again. He attacked the center of the board.

Sterling raised an eyebrow; Tim could tell that his opponent was being forced to think through his move or the first time in the game. Pondering the board, he licked his teeth. Tentatively, he made his move.

'Drip' went the clock.

Timothy heard voices echoing in his mind, bypassing his ear. Closing his eyes, he saw the figures struggling to reach his game.

'Drip' went the water.

"I say, Danforth. Shift that pipe there. I believe it will hold the load." The elderly man struggled to hold the debris blocking the passageway.

The younger pushed a large corroded pipe with his shoulder. "I'm trying, sir." Chunks of rotted wood groaned, shifting as the large lever did its job. Once the pipe was propping up the bulk of the debris, Professor Dyer leaned forward, jamming it against the wall. The way was cleared enough to get by.

The two men, teacher and student, squeezed through the makeshift way carefully stepping over the detritus littering the floor.

Holding their lanterns aloft, both looked at the passage before them. The runes and pictographs on the walls were getting cleaner, clearer. Less debris littered the way before them.

The passage stretched two hundred feet ahead. Green, discolored stonework across the walls from the corner. It would take only another ten or twenty minutes to work their way to hall's T-shaped turn Dyer breathed in deeply, steeling his nerves.

'Drip' went the water.

"Hahahahahahaha!" The voice wasn't loud, but still echoed. "You cannot win with that! You might as well give up now."

Danforth reached out, concern crossing his strong, chiseled features at his elder companion's reaction to the inhuman voice. "Are you sure you are up to this, Professor? Last time ...."

Dyer patted the younger man's shoulder. "Quite right, my young companion. Last time was bad. I daresay though, that the physics given me at Bethlam have restored my mental constitution. We must face the shoggoth and stop its perfidious machinations."

"I know, Professor. Truly I do. I fear that for you to gaze upon that which stole your sanity before shall strip it away again, this time sundering it permanently."

The older man pulled a handkerchief out of his breast pocket, wiping at his sweaty jowls. "We must. What lies beyond the chamber is the slow end to all we know. It must be stopped."

Danforth shook his head. "I don't understand, still. We are in an ancient chamber, sir. When last we were here, and faced the shoggoth, nothing else lived besides the food."

"What lies beyond is not alive or dead, Danforth. It slumbers, and has for millennia. This was revealed when the madness overtook me." He dabbed at his sweaty forehead.

The two moved forward to the next pile of rubble and began to shift debris. Leather protected their hands from the splintered wood and jagged corrosion of torn metal blocking the corridor. By inches the green glow pushed into the passage.

'Drip' went the water.

"Piece by piece I'll take you apart and put you back together. Piece by piece

your center will be mine. Piece by piece till no peace is known." The ethereal voice whispered, a susurrus creeping through the ancient underground city.

'Drip' went the water.

Leather, followed by skin, parted as a sharp rock punctured Danforth's hand. "Damn!" he sucked air between his teeth and shook his hand. Droplets of blood splattered on the wall, immediately vanishing as the hungry passage soaked it up.

"Tsk." Professor Dyer looked upset, bushy gray brows drawing together as he stared at his companion with consternation.

"What is it, Professor?"

Dyer grabbed the rock, flipped it over, and revealed the smooth underside. Sigils were etched on the surface, surrounding a pictograph of a man bleeding from his wrists. "I am afraid, dear boy, that you have unknowingly fed the Sleeping One. We must hurry, it has begun."

Danforth blanched. "I am sorry, sir. I shall make haste forthwith." Thinking quickly, he tied his kerchief around the wound and began moving the rubble again.

'Drip' went the blood.

The midgame was visceral. Both players had been stalwart in their defenses, building strong structures before moving to the actual battle.

The banter between the two had slowed, then eventually ceased completely; focus was applied more and more to the game. Sterling slid another piece, taking a rook.

'Click' went the clock.

"Damn!" Tim thought he heard the voice on the edge of hearing, but was too wrapped up in his strategy to pay attention. He played, ignoring the hanging bishop to attack the queen instead.

Sterling grunted. He was forced to move his queen out of the fray, to a more defensive position, or risk losing the game. He moved the piece back, baring teeth in a silent snarl.

Tim pushed his advantage, still ignoring the bishop attack in favor of developing a stronger position. Moving his knight in from the edge squares, he cornered his opponent's king. "Check."

Analyzing the board, Sterling raised an eyebrow. He slid his king to one side, but held onto the piece, still thinking. The board was ...

tricky. Every corner held a trap, threatened an exchange of pieces.

The question wasn't if battle would happen, but which fight he wanted to pick. Exhaling, Sterling released his grip on the king.

Tim grinned, picking up his knight and hammering it down onto the bishop's square, deftly swapping the pieces. Now he had support for the knight, and had revealed another attack on the queen.

'Click' went the clock.

The glow pulsed. Forms in the center of the chamber resolved as the shadows faded. Statuary, set into the walls of the chamber, seemed to all reach towards the center.

None of them were human, nor were they beast. Rather, they were something ... other. Standing erect, as man, they had the heads and arms of reptiles, amphibians, and things straight from the nightmares of ancient cave dwellers.

Each radiated a certain hunger, despite a composition of stone.

'Drip' went the blood.

Along the passage's walls, hidden channels in the stonework lit red, casting a deadly pallor along the ancient underground tunnel. Dyer and Danforth stopped, staring at the revealed patterns.

Red, glowing line-work revealed primitive patterns, pictographs of eldritch composition. Some depicted human sacrifice, others showed rulers, the Elder Things, being paid homage.

"What is this?" Danforth gulped, trying to keep calm.

Professor Dyer tossed a piece of wood aside, studying the final twenty feet of obstructed passage. "These are the rites of awakening. Those glyphs back there at the beginning of the passage took place long ago. They represent the rites of beginning." He pointed to the initial sacrificial pictures.

"Rites of beginning allowed the Elder Things their power here. They had ancient machinery, I believe, powered by slave blood." Both men continued to work on clearing the path, through the professor's explanation.

"Of course, by slave blood, I do mean human blood. As with the very stone that cut your hand, dear boy, I believe that each of these pictures of sacrifice is like our lamps, and blood the fuel which soaks the wick." Danforth listened raptly while making a path forward for them.

The Professor, as was the habit of a lifetime, continued to teach. "As you move along, you see the scenes of worship?"

Danforth grunted, sliding aside a particularly large piece of masonry, but managed a rasped, "I do."

"Very good," continued Dyer. "The blood powers the ancient machinery, but I believe that the worship grants a differing type of power to the Elder Things. Of course, I do not mean that it gains power such as a priest or politician, but rather that it gains an actual manifest energy through the worship. If I am correct, it is the selfsame power with which they created the shoggoth."

Colored lights mingled as the two shifted rubble, struggling forward, ever closer to the chamber. Green and red mixed to infuse the air with a sickly glow.

'Drip' went the blood.

"It won't be enough for you to win. Can't you see you've lost? You have lost it all." The two men had gotten used to the unearthly voice, and were, in the main, *ignoring it. Both had realized there was nothing they could do to understand what it was talking about; at least until they actually reached the chamber.*

'Drip' went the blood.

Danforth paused. "Professor, do you by chance understand any of the sigils?"

The aging scholar shook his head in regret. "That is where my knowledge fails me. My time of madness revealed certain things to me but ..." he paused, thinking through how to express his thoughts. Dyer scratched his chin. "The madness taught me a way of looking at the world. It did not impart knowledge, mystic or otherwise, on me. More, the remnants allow me a certain way of looking at the world."

Danforth shifted a final piece of rubble, leaving one final barricade before the chamber. He stopped and, as the Professor watched, drank deeply from his canteen. "Yet this other way of seeing the world does not instigate a return to the madness? Forgive me, Professor, for being so inquisitive. But I know so little of you, despite our previous journey to the ruins here."

Allowing the younger man a brief respite, Dyer talked while working on clearing the entryway to the chamber. "Of course, my lad.

The simplest answer is that no, I do not fear a return of the madness, so long as I take my physic every day."

The last pieces of the rubble fell away as they cleared the chamber's entry. Professor Dyer and Danforth stepped forward into the chamber.

'Drip' went the blood.

Two players stared at each other across a field of battle. Few of the warriors still stood. While each had started with an army of sixteen, each had but six left.

Tim stared. The pressure was back. Scratching at his temple, trying to relieve it, he avoided his opponent's stare. He scratched harder until the pressure was gone. His hands came away red and sticky, though he didn't show any outwards signs of caring.

He rocked back and forth. Every forced line ended in mutually assured destruction. There was no win here, but a tie. Playing a second game was not the plan.

Tim knew that repeating this game would break him mentally, probably forever. Line after line played out in his mind, looking for a solution. There wasn't one.

Sterling, his opponent, too closely matched his capabilities and style. This unknown had left Tim a wreck.

He had to find a way out. Trembling, he scratched at his temple.

'Drip' went the blood.

Danforth pulled a torch out of his rucksack. Kneeling down, he opened the cage of the lantern and tipped it to expose the flame. He lit the torch, carefully watching the shadowy glow.

The torch caught, but didn't pierce the shadows. Professor Dyer stood over him, staring at the room. "We must be cautious, though still make haste, young Danforth. We are almost out of time."

'Tick' went the clock.

"Indeed, Professor. Can you start handing me torches, please?" The two worked together, lighting torches quickly and efficiently. As each lit, Danforth would toss it into the chamber.

They were making good progress turning back the oppressive weight of the unnatural shadows, orange from the torches amplified the glows, both red and green.

Ambient light and shadows formed living walls, combating the light cast by the torches. The walls of the room were now visible. At consistent spacing of about ten feet there were large alcoves. Each contained a reaching statue of an Elder Thing, grotesque horrors with tentacles and gaping maws.

The professor spoke as they continued to light the torches. "I believe in the center of the room we shall find the shoggoth. Perhaps we can discover some truths about it ... but whether we do or no, are you ready to combat it?"

"I am." He was the only student interviewed who had not succumbed to the hypnosis techniques utilized by the legendary Herr Doctor Freud on his visit to Miskatonic University. Danforth had utilized a mental exercise proposed by Doctor Jung to great effect.

Both men believed that if anyone could resist the guardian shoggoth, and entity of smoke and shadows, which drove those who observed it mad, it would be Timothy Danforth.

The shadows finally fell under the incessant torchlight, revealing a frozen tableau in the center of the room, just as the unearthly voice spoke. "Stalemate."

'Tick' went the clock.

Timothy Danforth froze, taking in the scene before him. It wasn't possible ... how could this be?

'Drip' went the blood.

Tim Danforth froze, his hand hovering over the final move. This would finish it. A draw. Sticky warmth dripped down his face. Wiping at it, he blinked blood out of his eyes. The pressure was almost completely gone.

Thick, red life's blood dripped from his fingers as he reached across the board, playing his final move.

'Click' went the lock.

Green and red blended, the room filling with a purple luminescence as the mosaics all glowed into life. There were two figures in the center of the room, one standing, the other prone on the floor lifeless.

The standing figure moved. The room to burst into light in response. The two were on a grid, eight squares by eight, each grid square containing a hole in the center. Otherworldly figures, clones of the statuary in the perimeter alcoves, were locked into place on the platform. Many more of the statues, a couple dozen, littered the space next to the grid. Blood was everywhere in the center of the room, spilled from corpse and Tim alike.

Danforth blinked. He was immobile, fear freezing his feet. A hum sounded softly from the walls, and a vibration resonated beneath his frozen feet. The bleeding man was staring at him. Now that the final piece was in place, he rocked back and forth, whispering 'stalemate' over and over.

The hum was getting louder. Timothy Danforth remained rooted. He stared at Dyer, lying dead and drained of blood across the grid. He stared at himself, standing in the center of the grid, covered in blood, chanting stalemate.

His fingers were torn, the nails gone. Great swaths of skin on his face had been scratched away. He was ... emaciated. Haggard. As though he was decomposing while still alive. Somehow, he was both the man walking into the chamber, but also the half-dead man standing in the center of the room.

An otherworldly voice—feminine and soft while still not belonging in this reality—spoke from the walls of the room. "CTHULHU DRIVE ACTIVATED. TRANS-DIMENSIONAL ARK BOOTING. SEQUENCE ONE INITIATED. HUMAN-SHOGGOTH CONVERSION FINALIZING. PLEASE WAIT."

Danforth's bladder released. He understood the individual words, but not what the voice was saying. Adding to his confusion ... how he could be watching himself in the center of the room? Was it some trick? Some man that looked like him? Some double or shadow?

A trick of the shoggoth? Surety that the shoggoth was not tricking him, that he was two people at once, firmed itself in his mind. As the urine warmed his leg he finally let go of the traces of sanity piercing the confusion in his mind, and collapsed.

Tim Danforth blinked, trying to clear the blood from his eyes. The room was glowing, but the other him didn't matter. The game. Yes. The game. "Stalemate. Haha. Stalemate."

The chessboard was huge now, at his feet in the chamber. His opponent lay lifeless across the board. "Told you, you couldn't win! haha! haha. ha. Stalemate!"

Sucking on his finger, Tim let the warm taste of blood please his belly. He rubbed his leg. It was warm too. Rubbing the warmth, the wetness, soothed him. Shadows swirled around him, inching through his skin a pore at a time.

He continued to rub at his thigh with one hand while sucking blood off the other. The room looked different now. Colors were prettier. Blood tasted good. Smells, nidorous before, were soothing now.

"Shoggoth host detected. Genome map overlay commencing." Pretty voices were back, talking to him out of the air.

Cocking his head to the side, he pulled hand from mouth to point at Professor Dyer's corpse. "I won, you know. I played the game and won, you condescending bully!"

Spittle flew from his mouth. "I know it was a draw, but I won! See? All the pieces are in the right places!" He slapped at the button on the side of the grid. The one closest to him depressed as his bloody hand impacted it.

'Tick' went the clock.

'Drip' went the blood.

'Click' went the lock, for the final time.

"Gene splicing initiated."

Timothy Danforth crumpled as a red glow enfolded him gently. Consciousness slipped away. The human body melted into itself, losing tone and color until it was a black mass. Tentacles reached out of the mass, absorbing the chess piece keys to the outer seal.

The black mass grew. Beneath its undulations, the seal glowed. Quite suddenly, the lights in the chamber shifted to blue. Changing in form, the shoggoth seemed to fold in on itself. The shape of a human began to reemerge from the mass. Eyes glowed red as it sucked in air, looking once more like Tim Danforth.

Reaching down to the dead form of Dyer, the shoggoth Tim Danforth stroked the professor's temple. Knowledge flowed from the corpse to the hybrid beast. The guardian was finally fully constructed, ready to venture out into the world of men.

1956

Miskatonic University

"Now class. A demonstration of practical archeology." Professor Danforth reached under his desk, hefting a box onto the desk. The undergraduates were all eager to see what treasure he would show them.

"Can I get a volunteer?" he searched the young faces in the class. A straight-haired young man, a prodigy of the intellect, raised his hand. Fully five years younger than the rest of the young adults in the classroom, he was always eager to be learning, to interact.

Danforth smiled. "Young Mister Fischer. Excellent. Please come up here and hold open the box while I lift the relic out."

As the child prodigy, Robert Fischer, walked to the front of the classroom, Danforth explained, "This relic is masonry from a lost city. It was the final expedition of Miskatonic's Professor Dyer. He was a close friend, and I miss him every day. Observe."

Revealing the piece of masonry, Danforth lifted the relic. Every eye was glued to him, and the classroom began to glow red.

Peter J. Wacks, *throughout the course of his life, has been an actor, a designer of games and writer of accompanying story-lines, a writer of novels and other fiction, and a Bram Stoker Award nominee for his first graphic novel. Currently, he is the managing editor of Kevin J. Anderson and Rebecca Moesta's WordFire Press. He has been a panelist at over a hundred conventions and been a guest speaker at the GAMA Trade Show, Mensa, and UCLA. You can discover more about Peter at PeterJWacks.com.*

From the Author: "We've all heard the tall tales of writers creating their works based on bets. Heinlein, Hubbard, Asimov, even Butcher in the modern era have such tales centered around them. In this case, I have to thank (in alphabetical order, of course) Guy Anthony De Marco, Travis Heermann, and Vivian Caethe for making 'the bet' with me, and each other. In the case of this story, it was a lot of fun to research and write.

"I drew my inspiration for 'In the Move of Madness' from several sources. Most notable, of course, is the H. P. Lovecraft story for which this piece is named, and the characters drawn from. The particular story, as published, blazed the trail for the concept of Ancient Astronauts. As I happened to be watching the Ace Rimmer episode of Red Dwarf ... it seemed a natural fit to make my Ancient Astronauts dimensional travelers.

"Also notable, though, is the fascinating life and career of Bobby Fischer, a genius who passed the line into apparent madness, at least in the public eye.

"The game in this story is from 1967 between Fischer and Myagmarsuren. The original did not end in a stalemate, but then again, I didn't think that Danforth would play the line to as successful a conclusion as Mr. Fischer."

"Why aren't you studying, Vasili?" his father asked, looming over him like a bear as Vasili sat by the window. The silent snow fell outside in randomized patterns that had nothing to do with chess. He had studied for months now, enough to make him sick, enough to make his fingers ache at the very thought of picking up a chess piece.

"Mama said I shouldn't," Vasili said. Young children, she had told his father, should run and play, not study chess until their eyes burned. She had said it even on her deathbed, her rosary clutched in her thin hands.

Vasili ran the beads of his mother's rosary through his fingers. His father's anger burned behind Vasili like a furnace, even in the small confines of their apartment. Tiny and stoically Soviet, their apartment walls were bare of the decorations his mother had once hung so carefully, taken down by his father after her death. He never spoke of it, but Vasili suspected that his father could not stand to look at the religious icons and triptychs that his mother had so treasured.

"There is no place in the Soyuz for people who don't work, who don't study," his father said. "Your mother has made you weak. When you come to work at Chernobyl, you will see what being a man in the Soyuz means."

Vasili bit back a sigh. His father took him to the power plant at least once a month, determined to prepare him for his future work as a power plant operative. Vasili wanted to be a priest, like his father's brother, killed before the *Glasnost* by the secret police. Becoming a martyr and bringing the faith to the people was his sure ticket to heaven where his mother now lived.

Chess wouldn't get him ordained. Schoolwork would. His mother had made him promise to study hard and get top marks so he could

45

go into the seminary in Europe. He had promised her he would, but that hadn't meant anything about chess. Chess was only important if he wanted to be a man like his father.

"Study." His father threw a chess book at him. "Study and do well tomorrow. Or else."

Looking out the window, Vasili prayed he would lose, if only to spite his father.

The clock on the wall of the auditorium ticked away, the second hand jerking from one place to the next as Vasili stared at it instead of the board. Planted firmly in the center of the industrial green stripe on the upper part of the walls yellowed with the smell of sweat and the stagnant odor of cigarettes, the clock resolutely ticked on. Close to five hundred people had assembled to watch this chess match.

Mykola, his opponent, smirked and put his arm over the back of his chair as he kicked his feet, shoes squeaking on the linoleum. "Your turn, Peaceful Vasili."

Vasili hated the nickname the other kids had given him to mock his father's occupation with the "peaceful atom." The other kids' fathers worked at the power plant too, but none of them were so occupied with it as Vasili's father. None of the other kids had to go home at night to study schematics, to learn in detail their fathers' work. Vasili's father said it was necessary that he walk in his footsteps. His father hated the priesthood.

His hand hovered over a knight. His classmate had begun with a Russian Opening, and the crowd had sighed in appreciation. Vasili had countered it easily, but that didn't mean that Mykola wasn't playing him as much as the game. Ignoring his opponent, Vasili tried to read the patterns on the board. Maybe there would be a sign that he was to run away and join the priesthood. Maybe losing this game would provide the opportunity he needed. Perhaps his father would give up on him being a man like him. His father hadn't been able to attend the game; he wouldn't see what Vasili was doing. After he lost, he could go home and say, "Father, I wasn't able to win, I'm sorry" without his father knowing he had deliberately lost the game. It was only a white lie. Surely God would forgive him.

Moving his knight to match Mykola's, he folded his arms.

Vasili said his mother's prayers silently. *Hail, holy Queen, Mother of Mercy, our life, our sweetness, and our hope. To thee do we cry, poor banished children of Eve. In the name of the Father, the Son and the Holy Spirit, amen.*

Mykola raised his hand and held it hovering hovered it over a pawn. He stuck his tongue out at Vasili and moved a bishop instead.

There was something on Mykola's hand, a symbol that shimmered in the cold, winter sunlight that cascaded through the high windows of the auditorium. Vasili blinked as the board gleamed as if in resonance. The pieces shuddered as if jostled by a tremor.

The game progressed, and the worn and battered pieces wavered under Vasili's eyes. Mykola frowned at the board, whispering something under his breath. The crowd around Vasili took up the whisper, but surely it was his imagination.

The hair on the back of Vasili's neck itched as if someone blew on it. His opponent didn't seem to notice the pieces moving toward the center, improbably forming a spiral. Vasili tried to take the bishop with his pawn, but his hand went to the rook of its own accord. The sound of whispering intensified.

Sweat broke out on his forehead, and waves of heat crashed through him. He desperately blinked his eyes, trying to concentrate, trying to break free of this strange stagnancy. His opponent sweated as well as he tried to make his pieces move. His hand raised, Mykola tried to take Vasili's queen. Jerking to a pawn instead, he moved it toward the center of the board. His frightened gaze met Vasili's. He had stopped murmuring.

There was only one piece remaining outside of the spiral. Vasili reached toward it, the movement shuddering through his entire body, and tried to challenge the king. Vasili tried to resist it, but his arm betrayed him. It dropped the piece toward the last place in the spiral.

The piece fell into place, and silence filled the auditorium.

Brilliant, green light shot from the board, and Vasili cried out, freed from whatever strange effect the game had taken on him.

Released, he crashed to the floor as something howled with the sound of a thousand tormented souls. Righting himself, he made the sign of the cross and hoped no one noticed. He would be punished if he was caught being religious. There was no religion in the Soyuz and especially not in Pripyat.

The citizens' gazes fixed on the board as it slowly rose and rotated to the vertical, the pieces remaining as if forged there. The light in the citizens' eyes shone with reverence.

A void opened up above the board, shimmering with fluid blackness that swallowed up the green light, beating back its effervescence. The assembled citizens chanted strange words: *Ph'nglui mglw'nafh Cthulhu R'lyeh wgah'nagl fhtagn! Ph'nglui mglw'nafh Cthulhu R'lyeh wgah'nagl fhtagn! Ph'nglui mglw'nafh Cthulhu R'lyeh wgah'nagl fhtagn!*

The sound of the words turned his bowels. Gasping, Vasili wet himself and tried to scrabble away from the center of the room. Mykola stood, his face blank, his mouth moving to the sounds. The chubby teenager raised his arms as if in supplication and spoke aloud: *Ph'nglui mglw'nafh Cthulhu R'lyeh wgah'nagl fhtagn!*

Vasili prayed silently as he crossed himself again, not caring if they saw him. *Hail holy Queen, mother of God protect us sinners now and at the hour of our death, Amen.*

A horrible groping sensation filled his mind as tears streamed down his face. Something screamed in the periphery of his hearing, and the sensation left him sobbing.

The eerie sound of the chanting grew louder and louder.

The people of Pripyat turned toward him, their eyes alight with green luminescence as they pointed at him. *Ph'nglui mglw'nafh Cthulhu R'lyeh wgah'nagl fhtagn!*

Vasili swallowed. They knew. They knew about his faith, about how he wanted to be a priest, how he didn't want to learn chess.

Spiraling outward like a pinwheel, the void grew with every rotation. The chess board at the very center shattered, the pieces caught up in the maelstrom. Things moved within the void, horrifying shapes, frighteningly meaningless shapes.

A double-elbowed arm, shimmering with black and white scales, pushed, claws first, out of the void. Another arm followed it, then another and another. Unaware that he had even moved, Vasili caught up against the back of the auditorium stands, desperate to get as far away from the thing as possible.

The four-armed creature forced its head out of the void, mandibles dripping with ichor. Extending from a lizard head, skin stretched taut over the meter-long jaws that opened and closed as if hunting a scent. It looked down on him and clicked its jaws together.

Stepping from the void, the creature straightened to a full three meters, its entire body reptilian but for the mandibles and its round-pupiled eyes. It had a long tail that thrashed back and forth as it regarded the room. Its checkered, white and black scales shimmered, oily in the overhead lights as it cocked its head.

The glint in the creature's expression reminded him of his mother's stories of the demon Chernobog; it reeked of dead fish and sulfur. He crossed himself again, and the creature snorted. It turned its dark gaze to the standing people, all still chanting. The relief of not having its gaze upon him made his heart stutter. *Hail, holy Queen, Mother of Mercy, to thee do we cry, poor banished children of Eve.*

The creature strode to where Mykola stood and touched his chest with a clawed finger before opening its jaws wide. Slamming them closed, it severed Mykola's head from his torso. Blood spurted from the headless corpse to the beating of his heart. Wedged between the creature's mandibles, the head screamed silently.

Dropping the head, the creature howled. And from the depths of the rift, a howl returned.

Vasili stood on shaking feet and ran. The religious medals his mother had given him for luck clicked against each other under his shirt. *Hail, holy Queen, Mother of Mercy, to thee do we cry, poor banished children of Eve.*

The creature howled and gave chase. He dashed to the entrance of the school and out into the cold April morning. God would save him, if only he got to his father, if only ....

He dashed through knee-deep snow to his bicycle. The creature howled again as he rushed toward the only place he thought of as safe.

He clambered on the rickety bicycle and pedaled faster than he ever had down Lenin Avenue toward the power plant.

Howling grew closer behind him as his lungs ached from the cold air. There was no time to think, to plan, to outmaneuver it. All he could do was run.

The creature's footsteps thumped behind him. Over the exertion of his breathing and the squeak of the bike chain, the sound of the creature's feet sizzling on the snow followed him.

Close to three kilometers away, the power plant had never seemed so small or distant. He stood in his pedals, pushing himself faster than he had ever gone before on his bicycle.

His breath ached in his lungs as he passed the edge of Pripyat and went over the bridge where he and his father used to feed the fish in the summer. The road was clear, empty of the trucks and cars that normally crowded it. Something had changed here, there was something wrong. Had the creature taken the entire population under its spell?

Surely not. The guards at the power station would be able to help, would be able to stop the creature. Vasili's father would know what to do.

He rode down the asphalt access road, trying to block out the clacking of the creature's mandibles behind him. No matter how fast he pedaled, he couldn't out out-distance the creature.

The power plant loomed nearer, its steam rising to the sky. He gasped for breath.

Drawing close to the perimeter, he waved one of his arms at the guards, holding desperately onto the handlebars with the other. They raised their guns, then lowered them. "What's wrong, *malyutka?*"

"The ... creature ...." He gasped for air, then fell from the bicycle.

"What are you doing here, Vasili?"

"The chess game ...." Vasili caught his breath. "It came out of the chess game."

A howl shattered the afternoon. One of the guards gasped, while the other's hand twitched as if he wanted to make the sign of the cross. They both raised their Kalashnikovs.

He dashed through the front doors. Slamming them shut, he leaned against them. Barely daring to look, he nevertheless peered through the windows. The creature approached the men. It was even more horrifying in the spring daylight than it had been in the auditorium.

Turning away, he covered his ears. The gunfire and screams spurred him on. He dashed down the hallway, up the stairs and to the Gold Corridor, the central part of the power station. *Hail holy mother, Queen of heaven, protect us now and at the hour of our death.*

Vasili dared not look back.

Tripping, he fell and hit his knee. Tears came to his eyes as he stumbled back to his feet.

The creature's shadow moved across the windows. *Shccch shccch.* It ran its claws over the glass, searching for a way in. It would kill him. He knew it as certainly as the look it had given him when it came out of the chessboard.

It would kill him like it had killed Mykola.

He wasn't sure why it wanted him, why it chased him. Surely he wasn't the only one in the town that it wanted to kill? All the others had known the chant, had known what to say. But it hadn't spared Mykola.

Vasili got to his feet, the schematics of the building scrolling through his head like chess moves. It would be a straight shot to the control room, but if he could do it and outrun the creature, then there was a chance of trapping it in one of the secure reactor rooms. His father would know what to do with it from there. He ran.

The creature's footsteps followed him, its clawed feet clacking on the linoleum floor. Fear drove Vasili onward, fear and hope. *Holy Mother, Mary Queen of heaven, protect your servant.*

Vasili skidded around a corner and into the control room where his father worked with two other men. His father asked, "What are you doing in here, Vasili?"

Gasping he tried to gather the words to explain. "The chess game, Father, it came out of the chess game. It made us do it."

Vasili slammed the door shut and jumped to smash the security bar into place. In its rush forward, the creature hit the steel door, denting it. Despite the attack, the door held.

51

"Get away from the door, Vasili!" His father dragged him back.

Crooning, the creature made its way around the control room and to the floor below.

"Why did you do it, Vasili?" his father asked.

"Do what, Father?" Vasili frantically looked out the windows, trying to figure out where the creature had gone.

Vasili cried out as the crashed through hit the plate glass windows, shattering them. The workers stared in horror as the creature found its feet. The cry rose to their lips as well, the horrible words making Vasili gasp in fear. *Ph'nglui mglw'nafh Cthulhu R'lyeh wgah'nagl fhtagn!*

The creature turned its head right and left, torn between Vasili and his father and the workers. Impossibly fast, the creature went after one of the workers, knocking him hard into the wall. The man's head cracked against the cement, leaving a trail of blood as he slumped to the floor.

"You shouldn't have thrown the game, Vasili," his father said. "You were our hope, our last chance to defeat the evil that has been taking over our town. You, my holy child, were the last ray of hope. And now you have ruined it."

Vasili's heart pounded so hard in his chest that he couldn't breathe.

"Go, Vasili." Grimly, his father turned to the control panel and hit several buttons. Sirens shrieked through the power plant as the delicate controls were overridden by his father's commands. The worker reached for him, to stop him perhaps, but the creature turned at the noise, slashing out to catch his father in the back. Its claws tore through cloth and skin and to the soft intestines underneath. His father cried out, slumping over with pain.

The sirens shrieked louder as the smell of smoke assaulted Vasili's nose. The creature backhanded his father away from the controls, shrieking. It put its hands to its head, shaking it back and forth, blinking its eyes rapidly.

Vasili ran to the door, unbarring it. He must obey his father. He refused to look back.

He had to draw the creature down until there was no chance of it escaping to harm everyone else. His father could still be alive, if he could just stop this creature. Leaning over one another of the workers, the creature yanked open his chest with inhuman strength and consumed the organs one by one. Vasili stood in horror, then realized this was his chance. Perhaps the noise had distracted it from its single-minded pursuit of him.

Corridors flashed by him as he fled blindly. Without his father, Vasili didn't know what to do, how to fix this. The creature would eat him and they would win. He knew he should have obeyed his father, he should have been a good son, instead of selfishly following his own desires. God wouldn't want him if he was such a selfish brat.

Finding himself in the break area, he paused, confused. Why had he come here? Why hadn't he fled the building?

On the table of the break area was the battered chess set his father had brought in to practice with him. The chess game! If he could finish it, undo what had been done, then maybe the spell would be reversed. *Holy Mother, Queen of heaven, protect me now.*

Blinking rapidly, he laid the pieces out, desperate to find the same configuration as the board in the auditorium. Despite his hands' resistance, he persevered, moving the chess pieces one by one, remembering the movements from the game. Sweat broke out on his brow and he gritted his teeth against the creature's shrieks in the distance, growing closer. With his free hand, he grasped the medals under his shirt, praying with every ounce of his being. Surely if this creature was like Chernobog, then prayer would defeat it. *Holy Mother, guide my hand, protect us now and at the hour of our death!*

The surface of the board shuddered with unnamable colors, breaking down under his eyelids every time he blinked. He stood back and stared at it, refusing to let it bend his mind. He had to stop this; he had to stop it now. *Holy Mother, Queen of Heaven, protect your servant.*

The creature howled in the distance as it crashed into things. It was as if it was searching for him blindly now that it had lost sight of him. Wincing at the noise, he tried to focus.

Barely daring to breathe, he systematically began taking pieces. Pawns fell to kings fell to knights fell to queens fell to rooks fell to bishops fell to pawns. The cascade shook the board and the ground beneath the building quaked. The board rotated upwards, turning until it formed the portal again. Vasili braced himself, praying that he had done the right thing. If he had guessed wrong .... He didn't want to think about what would happen if he had guessed wrong.

The power plant sirens grew louder, then were silenced one by one.

In the silence that followed, the creature's footsteps came down the hall, sharp sharp-clawed feet clicking on the linoleum. He stood, ready to face it with the spiraling void of the portal behind him. He pulled his mother's religious medals from his shirt and held them out toward the creature. Perhaps God would forgive him for his pride, just this once.

Turning the corner, the creature approached him, its mandibles spread wide, its tail thrashing back and forth. It tensed, ready to pounce. Vasili prayed, finding no words left but the cry for his mother. "Holy mother, help me."

The creature leapt toward Vasili.

Falling to his knees, ready to die, Vasili clenched the medals in his hands and closed his eyes. The creature caught him around the waist and together they tumbled through the portal. Vasili smiled. He had done it. He had won the chess game.

Amen.

Vivian Caethe was introduced to speculative fiction at an early age while growing up in the Land of Enchantment. She writes on the side while sticking to her day job of telling people what to do and being mildly surprised when they comply. An avid tea connoisseur, she knits and cross stitches in her spare time.

The author of multiple short stories and novellas appearing in a variety of magazines and anthologies, Ms. Caethe writes in the constant search of "what if?" Her most recent endeavor, the novella series The Adventures of Vernon Auldswell Gentleman Explorer, is available through Bold Strokes Books.

In this short story, Ms. Caethe has delved into her lifelong obsession with Soviet-era Russia and what really happened at Chernobyl.

PATTERNS of THREAT

Travis Heermann

C atherine rubbed her eyes, and then flinched again at the swelling in both of them. The flinch sent fire through cracked ribs, into the brittle cauldron of her torso.

Had she seen what she thought she saw? A crack of light seeping between the black and white stone squares of the chess board?

She was losing it.

"Not enough sleep, Catherine," she mumbled.

Pink neon flashed steadily, inexorably, insomniacally through the window. Occasionally a half-garbled voice would filter up from the street, where just below her window the entrance of the twenty-four-hour pawn shop spilled wan fluorescence onto gum- and cigarette-spattered pavement. She could hear the meth and booze in the voices, bringing their latest stolen prizes for immediate cash, however pitiful the amount.

She opened the window and lit a cigarette, wrapping the threadbare chenille robe the house mother had given her tighter around her bony torso. The night breeze chilled her deeper than skin. The fresh air highlighted the haze of cigarette smoke and fear sweat trapped in her room, but it felt good, reminded her that she was still alive, that Jon could not reach her here. To have a room farther from the cesspit of human dregs below would have been preferable, but this was the last room in the shelter, unless she was willing to share. And right now, she needed some privacy and quiet more than anything.

Lightning limned the city skyline; an October storm was coming.

"Hey, mama!" a voice from below. "You selling? I'm buying!"

"Fuck off." She flicked ashes at him.

He gazed up at her from the recesses of a gray hoodie, hands thrust in his pockets, straggly red beard sprouting from the shadowed oval. "Come on now, don't be that way, mama. I got what you like."

On other nights she might have just closed the window, but tonight this lowlife felt like an insect that could not reach her. "Eat shit, thumb dick."

He stiffened and she caught a glimpse of jagged yellow teeth. "You think I don't know the way in there, bitch? You think you're better'n me?"

She sighed a cloud of nicotine bliss. Funny how she had had no interest in smoking until taking up with Jon. Her room was on the third floor, with nothing to climb between her and her admirer but a sheer brick wall. One last drag on the Salem menthol and she flicked it at him. It tumbled down, a spiraling trail of orange sparks, and her aim was true. He had to sidestep to dodge it.

He roared with rage, and a stream of foul vitriol vomited from him such as she hadn't heard since the last time she had seen Jon, two days ago. She sighed again and slammed the window shut.

She slumped beside the chessboard again, letting her mind slip into the lines and angles of threat and defense. Chess was the only thing that calmed her, forced her to think dispassionately, allowed her to put aside the incessant cascade of horrors her life had become. It had been her comfort in high school, as her mother had plunged off the high board into the deep end of a pool full of Stolichnaya. The fan rattled in the dented space heater in the corner, casting its toaster-orange glow toward her in the dimness.

A crash of glass showered her with cold razor splinters, and an empty bottle of rotgut whiskey shattered against the wall, gouging out a divot of age-softened plaster. Chilled glass talons fell into her hair, down her back. Screams of rage flew in through the shattered window like ebon-winged crows. She jumped to her feet and felt her soles pierced by glinting shards. She stripped off the robe, heard the tinkles of more shards on the floor, raked by tiny razors across her back, so sharp she hardly felt the slices until the blood began to flow. She stood there, frozen in shock and dismay.

A knock came at the door. Mrs. Hendricks' voice came with a hard challenge, "Everything okay in there?"

"Uh, not really ...."

"Don't you be breaking nothing in there!"

"Some lowlife douchebag outside threw a bottle. I'm surrounded by glass."

The house mother clucked her tongue in disgust. "All right, I'll bring you a broom."

Catherine brushed her fingers through her hair, and gasped as tiny fragments punctured and sliced. She stopped, and let her hands hang limp like some bleeding sacrifice.

The chess board sat below her, strangely beautiful, the faint whorls in the stone squares almost taking the shape of strange glyphs. Something niggled at the edges of her awareness, some pattern of lines and angles, incidence and intention, cause and effect initiated by the past and future movements of the pieces, openings and inevitabilities, if only she could grasp it. The pieces were cast in some bizarre metal that defied color, not pewter or brass or bronze, but their detail was striking in its baroque intricacy, as if each of them could launch into grandiloquent action of its own accord. The set was either extremely old or an excellent representation of antiquity. Spotting it in the dumpster behind the pawn shop her first night here had been an incredible stroke of fortune. Even if it were some recently manufactured trinket, the chess set had been a godsend to her mental well-being.

How does a high school chess champion, certified Master at age seventeen, full-ride scholarship winner, end up in a half-way house for battered women at age twenty-five? In part, by thinking that the wildly creative, wildly passionate, wildly exuberant—wildly moody—photographer, who was strangely interested in little Cathy, Bespectacled Nerd Girl Extraordinaire, who for the first six months of their relationship lit bonfires of ecstasy in every nerve-ending, and who, in the four and a half years since, had mastered pressing all of her deepest, darkest buttons, and who had, by imperceptible increments, stripped her of every friend, every modicum of joy, every sliver of her own identity, and replaced it with himself, replaced it with incredible adroitness at walking on eggshells and tightropes, replaced it with constant alertness for his wild oscillations between pitiful "poor me" neediness and irrational, incoherent rage, by thinking that he would be a man that would stay with her forever in dreamy bliss, as long as she could fix him.

Hands hanging limp away from her sides, jewels of deep scarlet growing upon them, she waited for Mrs. Hendricks to return. She would have to comb the glass out of her hair.

Footsteps approached in the hallway. "Lord A'mighty, girl. You a mess!" Mrs. Hendricks stood in the doorway, broom and dustpan in hand, surveying the glittering carpet of broken glass.

Catherine turned to look at her and felt a couple of blood droplets fall from her fingertips. With a gasp of worry that they might have fallen on her chessboard, she looked down, and thought for a moment that she saw droplets on one of the white squares and on one of the black squares. Then she blinked and the droplets were gone.

Mrs. Hendricks swept herself a path into the room, shaking her head and mumbling as she went on about "all the goddamn hoodlums" and "how they just do the same stupid shit over and over, thinking it's gonna be any different the next time, like they's going through the motions of life, you know?" and "people got to start caring and loving and thinking!"

"I have glass in my hair," Catherine said.

"Sakes alive, girl. You look a mess. Just stay there till I'm done sweeping."

The sound of a deep, thrumming hum rose from below her, growing louder and louder as Mrs. Hendricks swept, like the sound of an approaching freight train, if a freight train could play the pipe organ. The sound grew so loud, that it should have been vibrating the walls.

"What's that noise?" Catherine said. "Boiler or something?"

"I don't hear nothing. I ain't fired up the boiler yet this fall, gotta save the fuel for winter." Mrs. Hendricks dumped her dustpan into the trash bin.

The tremor of the hum seemed to change notes, like someone playing the biggest, sub-baritone pipe organ anyone had ever conceived.

"There," Mrs. Hendricks said, surveying the floor again. "I think I got it all. I'll fetch a rag to mop up the blood."

Catherine tried to give her a half-smile. "Got any band-aids?"

Mrs. Hendricks sighed again. "I'll see what I can do." She mumbled her way out. Her apartment was three doors down.

Catherine sat on the squeaky twin bed, having left a trail of bloody footprints from where she had been standing. She dug three shards of glass out of the bottoms of her feet, hissing with pain. A wet breeze and the sound of pattering rain wafted through the shattered window. The screaming outside had stopped.

Why her?

Jeremy, the first boyfriend she had had in high school—how ill-conceived that venture had been—had turned into a jealous maniac the first time another boy had smiled at her. Unused to all the unexpected attention, little Cathy had simply cringed into a hole, until she couldn't take it anymore, stopped returning his phone calls, and skipped school for a week. Those absences had cost her valedictorian. Twenty-seven unanswered phone calls in a single hour at the height of his craziness, while she simply rocked on the bed, her mother downstairs lost in vodka oblivion.

Mrs. Hendricks returned with a first aid kit and saw to Catherine's lacerations, clucking her tongue. "You hang in there, girl. The whole world ain't awful, no it ain't. You got to take a little time, get your head straight, take stock, you know? You a smart girl with your chess playing and such. Ain't bad to look at neither, for a skinny little white girl. You go back to your job yet?"

"I'm afraid he's staking it out." While Mrs. Hendricks wrapped Catherine's feet in gauze, Catherine combed the glass out of her hair.

"Don't he have a job to go to?"

"I've been supporting him for over a year. He blew up at his boss and got fired. This town isn't that big, I figure word got around."

"Well, you just hang in there. The Lord will provide. Just gotta have faith. There! Done all I can do."

Warmth wormed into Catherine's belly. "Thanks, Mrs. Hendricks."

"Call me Mabel."

"Thanks, Mabel. You saved my life again."

"That's what I'm here for. I'll be back in a jif with some plastic wrap and duct tape. Can't have it raining in."

Neon pink splashing rhythmically over her feet, Catherine lay in bed, bathed in the coal-orange glow of the space heater, listening to the rain patter against the window, the rustle of the plastic wrap taped over the window like a big patch of gauze as it sucked in and out with the wind. The wetness of cold October storms seeped into her bones. She huddled under meager blankets that smelled of industrial laundry products, shivering from more than the cold.

The cold, seething, bestial rage in Hoodie Man's voice struck some deep well of fear, and now it was gushing all over her. Jesus, was this what it was like to encounter pure evil, look into its eye?

Jon probably wasn't evil, just a weak, spineless piece of shit. With all his creative and photographic efforts falling into utter failure, the only way he could make himself feel like a man was to beat on her, emotionally for years, and now, finally, physically.

The heater's grille pattern stretched over the floor, drawing black lines across her body. She knew she must get some sleep. Tomorrow she had to go to the police and have them forcibly remove Jon from the apartment, and she didn't want to do it looking like a meth head herself. The fact that her life already looked too much like a stereotype lent its own flavor of bile to the repeating assembly line of emotions cycling through her. At least she had been smart enough to put the lease in her name. How much of her stuff had he destroyed in some fit of childish rage? It was not beyond his capabilities to burn the apartment and everything she owned to ground and, for extra bonus martyr points, himself in it. But he didn't have those kind of guts.

The tremendous subsonic hum she heard before had faded, but sometimes she thought she caught snatches of it in her bones and viscera, some discordant melody ghosting through the walls of this place.

A hundred-year-old floorboard creaked in the hallway. The thirty-year-old flip-dial clock on the dresser said 3:17. The crease of light under the door darkened with a shadow.

Was that a long, quavering breath against the door?

Her muscles tensed.

No way could that guy have gotten in, with massive steel doors and a twenty-four hour security guard downstairs. But she hadn't explored the entire building, the basement, the roof, the fire escapes.

Moments dragged past.

No one should be up and moving around at this time of night.

The doorknob rattled.

With another bloom of cold, sick dread in her belly, she realized that she had not replaced the chain lock after Mrs. Hendricks had left, and the doorknob lock was so old and sticky that it sometimes did not lock properly.

The doorknob rattled again, so quietly.

She launched herself out of bed and flung herself toward the chain.

A body shoved against the door.

Her bandaged fingers couldn't get a grip on the chain. Sobs of desperation flew out of her with each fumbling failure.

A voice outside, inches from her face. "I can smell you in there, bitch."

The doorknob cranked, hard. Something snapped and splintered.

The door burst in and slammed into her face. A spike of agony drove from her nose to her brain. Stars of pain flew into her eyes. Falling backward onto the chessboard, scattering the pieces. She tried to gather breath for a scream, but nothing would come. Hot saltiness poured across her lips.

Sodden with rain, the gray hoodie shadowed his face. Only his clenched, yellow teeth gleamed in the pink neon, surrounded by coarse bristles. He fell upon her, surprisingly light, but wiry as twisted springs.

"I told you I knew the way in here, bitch." He snatched both of her wrists and slammed them against the floor. His fetid breath blasted into her face. "Oh, yeah, I told you. Now we're gonna dance to the music." The red strands of beard fluttered so close they reached out to caress her cheek. "You hear it, donchoo! Oh, let's dance to it, baby!"

His knee against her belly drove the breath out of her in helpless puffs. She twisted her hands free, clawed at his face with one hand, the other closing around one of chess pieces. Instantly, she knew which one, the knight, with the strangely winged horse that somehow wasn't a horse, with upstretched wings and fierce countenance. She stabbed, raked, gouged the chess piece into his face. He howled with pain and laughter, and in that flurry of movement, his hood tore away.

It was then she screamed with everything she was worth.

His entire head was nothing more than pale flesh, blank as an egg, with only the drooling, yellow-toothed mouth, lips like a lamprey, and the beard that moved of its own accord, like a mass of filthy red feelers reaching for her face.

Her instincts latched upon a moment of opportunity and thrust a knee up into his groin, pummeling with all she had left. He registered no reaction. She kneed him again, as hard as she could, but felt as if her knee had just slammed into the flat, featureless crotch of a Ken doll.

She stabbed again with the knight's twin wings, now dark and wet with ... something.

Still, he laughed. A switchblade flicked open in his hand. In an instant of bizarre focus, her gaze slid from his no-face to the knife blade glinting with coal-orange. Swirls and whorls in the steel, jumping into her awareness spider-quick. Swirls and whorls in the chessboard, delicate patterns of making and unmaking, order and chaos.

Confusion swept the shards of rationality from her mind.

Her eyes caught the flicker of another shadow, her ears, the pounding of approaching feet.

From behind him, a hand, a snapping arc of blue electricity. The taser jammed into the back of his neck. His body convulsed, twisting backward into a spine-cracking arch. He flung himself upright, knees wobbly but shrugging off the stun charge like a bull, and turned on Mrs. Hendricks, whose eyes ballooned with terror.

Mrs. Hendricks hit him again with the taser, squarely in the chest, and this time, he dropped like a marionette with its strings cut. For good measure, she jabbed the taser onto the top of his naked pate and hit him again. He convulsed, and then lay limp, a wrung-out rag.

"Oh, yeah, you staying down, motherfucker! You staying down!

64

You staying down! You staying down!" Trembling and stamping, Mrs. Hendricks circled him like a half-crazed mother bear.

Catherine gasped and rubbed her swollen eyes. The face of the man on the floor had taken on a human look, complete with deep-shadowed eyes, shaved head, broken nose, and a junkie's sunken cheeks.

Mrs. Hendricks offered Catherine her hand. "What you looking at?"

"Nothing." She got to her feet.

In the hallway stood several half-clothed women, one carrying a baseball bat, another with a small chrome revolver. They hovered out there, ready to circle her for protection.

Clenched in Catherine's fist, something squirmed: the knight with blood on its wings. Jesus, what an overactive imagination.

Mrs. Hendricks called out in the hallway. "Abby, grab my zip ties from on top the fridge. Tiffany, call 9-1-1. The cops gonna deal with this motherfucker."

E very time the junkie so much as twitched, Mrs. Hendricks tased him again, until the cops finally arrived eight minutes later.

Catherine gave them her statement from deep in a fog. With the feeling of his knee still in her gut, she refused to go to the hospital, didn't have money or insurance to pay for it. The officers finally hauled him away by the arms, his smooth-worn Nikes dragging the floor. "Nice to see you again, Kenny," one of them said.

As the furor passed into vague, sick aftermath, the low-voiced comfort of some of the other women lent her a few shreds of strength. In their eyes, she saw horror, fear, respect, worry about whether they'd have had the strength to fight him off, and thankfulness that it hadn't been them.

When the door finally closed, she curled up in the corner, knees drawn to her chest, the plaster hard and cold against her back. Incessant rain pattered against the window. At 5:08 a.m., she stubbed out her last cigarette.

Something squirmed in her hand.

The knight. Had it been there all this time?

The humming had returned, at the bottom of her hearing.

Turning it over and over in her fingers, caressing it with her thumb, warm after so long in her grip.

She slid across the uneven floor and placed it on the board with a solid clack. She gathered up the pieces, lined them up, and played.

As the window faded to a dismal gray and sounds of rain-spattered traffic filled the silence, she played.

Jon stopped playing chess with her after she had beaten him one too many times while reading a book. She played her favorite openings, the Ruy Lopez, the Queen's Gambit, the Sicilian Defense, the Pirc Defense, seen by many as weaker but allowing black to feint and come back hammering white's position. The movement of the pieces picked up speed as she swept through game after game after game, the infinite variation of the universe at her fingertips. With four hundred different positions after each player's first move, 72,084 positions after two moves apiece, more than nine million positions after three moves apiece, more than 288 billion possible positions after four moves apiece, the possibilities of a single chess match exceed the boundaries of the universe. In only games of forty moves, there are more openings, defenses, gambits, possibilities than quarks in this universe, more unique game-trees than the number of galaxies.

The only meaningful impossibility in chess is for the game to end in simultaneous checkmate, two kings, black and white, each victorious, both defeated.

And she played and the hours fluttered past into darkness again, she was victorious as many times as she was defeated, each win tainted by failure. When she was younger, she could lose herself in the lines and patterns, so intensely focused that she even missed an entire day of school once to studying the intricacies of Byrne vs. Fischer, 1957, the Gruenfeld Defense with Three Knights Variation, the Hungarian Attack.

But Jon had "saved" her from her social ineptitude and introduced her to a bright and shining world of art and music, parties and pot. He had opened up her life, and then destroyed it.

Immersing herself in the patterns of the game, slowly other

patterns juxtaposed over the moves, all the millions of intricate decisions, surrenders, concessions, bargains, reducing the possibilities of choice. The choices of her life. The junkie, if that's what he had truly been. On an infinite board, with infinite squares, infinite numbers of kings and queens, pawns and knights, bishops and rooks, all lived and died, moved and remained quiescent, sought advantage and sacrificed themselves, all moved in patterns, all danced to the discordant melody and inexorable rhythm of some unseen flautist, a chorus of insane flautists piping for the amusement of ... what? Something larger than the universe itself?

Light seeps between the squares of the board as the pieces move. Battles are fought. Blood is spilled. Queens die, impaled on the lances (proboscises?) of winged knights. Bishops chant to their congregations of weak, frightened pawns, pawns that no less display incredible power when working in unison.

She cannot remember if she is still moving the pieces herself, noticing for the first time an uncanny gulf between her mind and her hands, but the games progress. Something watches her, touches, only barely noticed. The patterns repeat in endless spirals, patterns of her life, patterns of her actions, patterns of her choices, of her choices, her choices, choices. She is trapped in repeating patterns, defeats that look like victories, unnecessary sacrifices and meaningless gambits and endless appeasements. Again, her life there, a pattern on this infinite board, destined to repeat.

Until, like a door slamming open somewhere in the vast gulfs between galaxies, it happens.

Two kings, both checkmated.

She cannot wrap her mind around this. It is impossible. Reality tilts on an invisible axis. Her stomach heaves.

She backtracks through the moves, but cannot grasp where the game passed beyond the bounds of possibility.

The hum vibrates, but not from below her—she was mistaken—but from the board itself.

The window has grown light again.

There is pounding on the door.

"Open up, goddammit, or I'ma bust this motherfucker down!"

Suddenly, time-space itself was realigned. Catherine was still sitting on the floor. Her ass and feet were numb, her knees on fire, her fingers trembling, her head swimming in dizziness, her belly clutched in vague nausea.

Her voice came out a croak. "Just a sec!"

She tried to stand, couldn't, forced herself to crawl on all fours toward the door, used the door knob for a handle to pull herself upright.

"I know you in there! I heard you talking!"

Talking?

Catherine took a moment, a long deep breath, flexed her toes, her knees, rubbed her face—her hands stank of the strange metal of the chess pieces.

She opened the door.

At the sight of her, Mrs. Hendricks recoiled. "Lord have mercy, child. You better not be tweaking up in here."

Words felt strange coming out of her mouth. "No. Just. Thinking."

"You been gone for two days! Thought something mighta happened to you."

"No, I've been here the whole time."

"I let myself in yesterday to check on you, wasn't nobody here."

Catherine had no idea what to say to that. She could only let the silence hang and stretch.

"Anyway, I brung you some donuts and a cup of coffee." Mrs. Hendricks offered a paper bag and a styrofoam cup.

"Thanks." Catherine took them. The crinkle of the paper was a strange percussion to the hum still in her ears. "You sure you don't hear that? It's almost like music."

Mrs. Hendricks shook her head steadfastly. "Alls I hear is a girl about to find herself on the street if she don't get her shit together."

"Thanks for the donuts." Catherine's smile was a brittle facade. "You are a queen."

Mrs. Hendricks' bristling stiffness softened a bit. "Well." Then she departed.

Catherine closed the door and opened the bag. She wasn't hungry, but enough rationality had returned to tell her that she needed to eat something. The smell of sugar and raspberry filling wafted out, slid up her nose, and drove a fist of nausea into her belly. She ran for the trash pail and heaved a trickle of whatever was left in her stomach, long empty, over the glass shards. The convulsions continued until only dry retching remained, and she leaned her elbow against the wall, forehead resting on her arm.

Morning sky painted the plastic wrap with clear sunshine and the evermore familiar sound of morning traffic hummed, tires on pavement drifting in and out of strange harmonies.

She wiped her mouth and lay a hand on her belly, looked down at it.

No. It couldn't be.

How to break the pattern?

Introduce an impossibility. A miracle. A new piece.

Suddenly the patterns of life blasted through her conscious like a blaze of light.

In that instant, she snatched up the chess board, tucked it under her arm, swept the pieces into the donut bag, and, heedless that she had no idea how long she had been wearing the same clothes, went out onto the street, and walked toward the bridge. Traffic flowed and honked, burst and crawled and halted, all to endless rhythms unseen by everyone except her. Passersby stepped out of her path.

Each step took her further out of rhythm and harmony with the humming melody that would not leave her ears.

Standing at the rail of the bridge, she looked down at the great, muddy brown river, as relentless as the flow of time. She threw the chessboard over the side, watched it spin and arc like a frisbee until it smacked the water with an ignominious splash and sank out of sight. One at a time, the pieces followed, and each one she attempted to throw for greater and greater distance.

The bag empty of all but pockmarked donuts, she stood there, and drew a series of long, deep breaths. She would never play chess again. She wouldn't need to. The patterns of her life were emblazoned upon her mind like burnt circuits. But in so knowing, she could see them, avoid them.

The police station was only a little detour on the way back to the shelter. It was time to go home again.

Even though she hadn't had sex with anyone except Jon, somehow she could not be sure this baby was his. But it didn't matter. He would never know of its existence.

Travis Heermann is a freelance writer, novelist, award-winning screenwriter, editor, poker player, poet, biker, roustabout, graduate of the Odyssey Writing Workshop, author of the Ronin Trilogy, The Wild Boys, *and* Rogues of the Black Fury, *plus short fiction pieces in anthologies and magazines such as Innsmouth Free Press'* Historical Lovecraft, *Cemetery Dance's* Shivers VII, *and Fiction River's* How to Save the World. *As a freelance writer, he has produced a metric ton of role-playing game work both in print and online, including Legend of Five Rings, d20 System, and the MMORPG, EVE Online.*

He enjoys cycling, horror films and fiction, torturing young minds with otherworldly ideas, and zombies. He has three long-cherished dreams: a produced screenplay, a NYT best-seller, and a seat in the World Series of Poker.

This story came together from a several inspirations: the idea of an anthology to benefit shelters for battered women, and the author knowing personally more than one woman who has been physically and emotionally abused. He read a chilling statistic recently saying that abused women leave their abusers an average of seven times. Monsters lurk in those numbers.

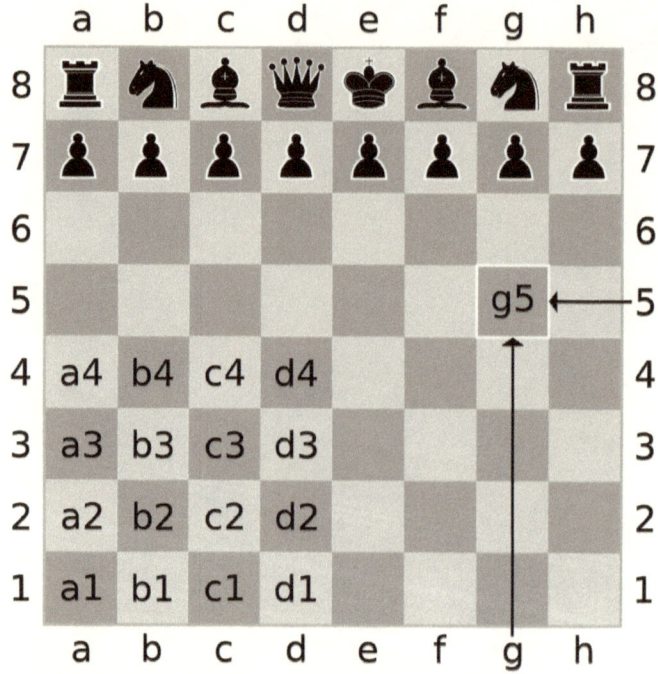

Image Source: Wikipedia, "algebraic notation".
File name: SCD_algebraic_notation.svg

Appendix: Chess Notation

A stute readers will notice that some of the stories in this anthology contain an arcane language, a bizarre, magical code that seems to have some consistency and meaning ....

That would be *algebraic notation*, the world standard notation for describing and recording the moves in a chess game. If you are a chess enthusiast or just a curious dabbler, you can recreate real chess games with this notation.

Squares on the Board

Like a Cartesian graph, squares on the chessboard are identified by a letter and a number, which form a unique coordinate pair. The vertical columns of squares are called *files*, and the horizontal rows are called *ranks*. From White's left (the queenside) to his right (the kingside), the files are labeled a through h. The ranks are numbered 1 to 8 starting from White's side of the board. Each square therefore has a unique identification consisting of file letter plus rank number.

Example: Black's king starts the game on square **e8**. *White's knight on* **b1** *can move to open squares* **a3** *or* **c3**.

On the opposite page is a representation of a chess board with algebraic notation added.

Names of Pieces

Each type of piece type, except for pawns, is identified by an uppercase letter corresponding to the first letter of the piece's name (however, this varies by language). In English-speaking countries, K indicates king, Q indicates queen, R indicates rook, B indicates bishop, and N indicates knight (since K is already used).

Pawns are identified by the *absence* of an uppercase letter. Since only one pawn can possibly move to a given square, distinguishing between them is unnecessary (with the exception of captures, discussed below).

Notation for Moves
Each move is indicated by the piece's uppercase letter, plus the coordinate of the destination square.

Example: Moving a bishop to e6 is notated as **Be6**. *Moving a knight to a3,* **Na3**. *Moving a pawn to e4 is simply* **e4**. *(Note the absence of the letter indicating piece.)*

Notation for Captures
In any given move, an "x" inserted immediately before the destination square indicates that a piece has been captured.

Example: A queen captures a piece on f4, resulting in a notation of **Qxf4**.

Pawns are a special case. A capturing pawn's starting file is used to identify the pawn.

Example: A pawn on the b-file captures the piece on c5, resulting in a notation of **bxc5**.

Variations on this notation sometimes use a colon (:) instead of *x*, either in the same location as the *x* (Example: **N:c5**), or at the end (**Ne5:**).

Pawns that capture *en passant* captures are similar to normal pawn captures, except that the capturing pawn's destination square is used (not the square of the captured pawn). A suffix of *e.p.* is occasionally used to show that the capture was *en passant*.

Move Clarification
It can happen that two or more identical pieces can move to the same

square. When this occurs, the notation begins with the moving piece's letter, then one of the following, depending on the circumstances:

1. If the files of departure differ, use the letter of the file.

2. If the files are the same, but ranks differ, use the number of the rank.

3. If neither rank nor file is sufficient to identify the piece, use both the file and rank. This only occurs when pawns have been promoted so that a player now has three or more identical pieces able to reach the same square.

Example: Knights occupy spaces g1 and d2. Both of them can reach f3. To indicate which knight moved, **Ngf3** *or* **Ndf3** *is used as necessary. If the knights occupy the same file, on squares e5 and e1, the moves are* **N5f3** *or* **N1f3**. *Again, when a piece is captured, an* x *is inserted (***N5xf3***).*

Example: Two rooks occupy d3 and h5. Either one can move to d5. If the d3 rook moves, file takes precedence over rank, so **Rdd5** *is correct. If the move is a capture,* **Rdxd5** *is likewise correct.*

Never let it be said that horror stories lack educational merit.

www.ingramcontent.com/pod-product-compliance
Lightning Source LLC
Chambersburg PA
CBHW020549130626
46552CB00007B/2831